W9-CCD-829

HOW TO USE THIS BOOK

Read the captions in the eight-page booklet and, using the labels beside each sticker, choose the image that best fits in the space available.

•

Don't forget that your stickers can be placed on the page and peeled off again. If you are careful, you can use your *Star Wars* stickers more than once.

•

You can also use the *Star Wars* stickers to decorate your own books.

LONDON, NEW YORK, MELBOURNE,
MUNICH, AND DELHI

First American Edition, 1999
Second American Edition, 2004
11 12 14 20 19 18 17
022 - SD156 - Aug/04

Published in the United States by
DK Publishing, Inc.
375 Hudson Street
New York, New York 10014

Copyright © 2004 Lucasfilm Ltd. and ™.
All rights reserved. Used under authorisation.
Page design copyright © 2004 Dorling Kindersley Ltd.

Written by Rebecca Smith
Edited by Jane Mason and Rebecca Smith
Designed by Kim Browne

All rights reserved under International and Pan-American Copyright Conventions. No
part of this publication may be reproduced, stored in a retrieval system, or transmitted
in any form or by any means, electronic, mechanical, photocopying, recording, or
otherwise, without prior written permission of the copyright owner.
Published in Great Britain by Dorling Kindersley Limited.

ISBN 978-0-7566-0764-7

Reproduced by Media Development and Printing Ltd, UK
Printed and bound by Thumbprints, Malaysia

Dorling Kindersley would like to thank
Lucasfilm for the photography.

www.starwars.com

Discover more at
www.dk.com

The Empire

From the moment the Emperor took control of the Old Republic, renaming it the Galactic Empire, the galaxy has been threatened by tyranny and evil. The Emperor ruthlessly uses the dark side of the Force to control his subjects. Protected by a vast army of lethal machines and sinister generals, he will stop at nothing to expand the realms of Imperial power.

Loyal Guard
Fanatically loyal, the mysterious Imperial Royal Guards protect the Emperor. They are highly trained in deadly arts and use vibro-active force pikes to inflict lethal wounds.

Dark Knight
Prowling the corridors of the Imperial Navy, Darth Vader is a much-feared military commander. He was once a pupil of the Jedi Obi-Wan Kenobi, but now works for the Emperor. Vader's knowledge of the dark side of the Force makes him extremely dangerous.

White Fighter
Highly disciplined and loyal to the Emperor, the stormtroopers are shielded by white space armor. They are the most trusted and effective troops in the Imperial military.

Lethal Weapon
Darth Vader's lightsaber has a blade of pure energy that can cut through nearly any object.

Head Protection
The Death Star gunner's helmet is fitted with a transceiver and a shielded lens.

Close shot
The standard blaster is issued to every scout trooper. This weapon is ideal for short-range targets.

Double Bomber
The Empire's main bomber is the TIE assault bomber. It is exceptionally successful on ground-bombing missions.

Evil Dictator
Drawing his powers from the dark side of the Force, the terrible Emperor rules the military forces of the Imperial Navy. His simple clothing and hood conceal his twisted features.

Accurate Shot
This rugged laser rifle has incredible consistency and accuracy.

Controlled Power
The lethal TIE Interceptor has dagger-shaped solar panels. It also has special ion drives that give the pilot extra control.

Lone Trooper
Scout troopers are trained to endure long periods without support. They are only armored on the upper body and head.

Torturer
The pitiless interrogator droid surgically exploits every weakness it finds in the enemy.

Terrorizer
These fearsome wedge-shaped warships are called Star Destroyers. They carry devastating firepower throughout the galaxy to terrorize any opposition.

Tough Walker
The gigantic All Terrain Armored Transport (AT-AT) walkers are invulnerable to most blaster bolts and cannons.

Agile Fighter
Small and fast, the TIE fighter is built for exceptional maneuverability.

Fast Walker
The All Terrain Scout Transport (AT-ST) is known as the scout walker. Fast and agile, it can travel over rough terrain in search of hidden enemy groups.

Ultimate Weapon
Invulnerable to large-scale assault, the Death Star contains a hypermatter reactor that can generate enough power to destroy an entire planet.

Stormtrooper Blaster
Compact and rugged, the E-11 BlasTech Standard Imperial sidearm combines excellent range with lethal firepower.

Probe Droid
Intelligent and eerie, the probe droid is equipped with myriad sensors and investigative instincts.

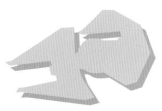

Galactic Life

The galaxy is teeming with mysterious creatures and beings. Many of these are outlaws, who try to survive beyond the Empire's grasp. Jawas trade in scavenged junk and droid parts; Jabba the Hutt masterminds a criminal empire all his own; and even musicians sometimes gamble their way out of debt. And then there are the bounty hunters, who thrive by their murderous and violent deeds.

Explosive device
Carried at the back of the belt, the thermal detonator contains powerful explosives.

Vile Crime Lord
Astute and ruthless, Jabba the Hutt is at the center of a large criminal empire. He eats nine meals a day and enjoys using his power and wealth to control weaker species.

Notorious Hunter
Cool and calculating, the mysterious Boba Fett is the best bounty hunter in the galaxy. He has his own code of honor and only takes on missions that meet his harsh sense of justice.

Swindler's Tool
Used by the swindling Jawas, ionization blasters feature built-in ion regulators and a blast nozzle.

Military Droid
The RA-7 Protocol Droid is a military model designed to work closely with the latest E-wing fighter.

Pleasure Craft
Jabba the Hutt's sail barge, *Khetanna*, is used to transport the crimelord wherever he wishes to go.

Musical Minds
Naturally musical and intelligent, the band called the Modal Nodes is the most often heard in the Mos Eisley Cantina. Their lead player, Figrin D'an, is an experienced gambler who manages to keep the band out of trouble.

SPACECRAFT, VEHICLES, DROIDS & EQUIPMENT

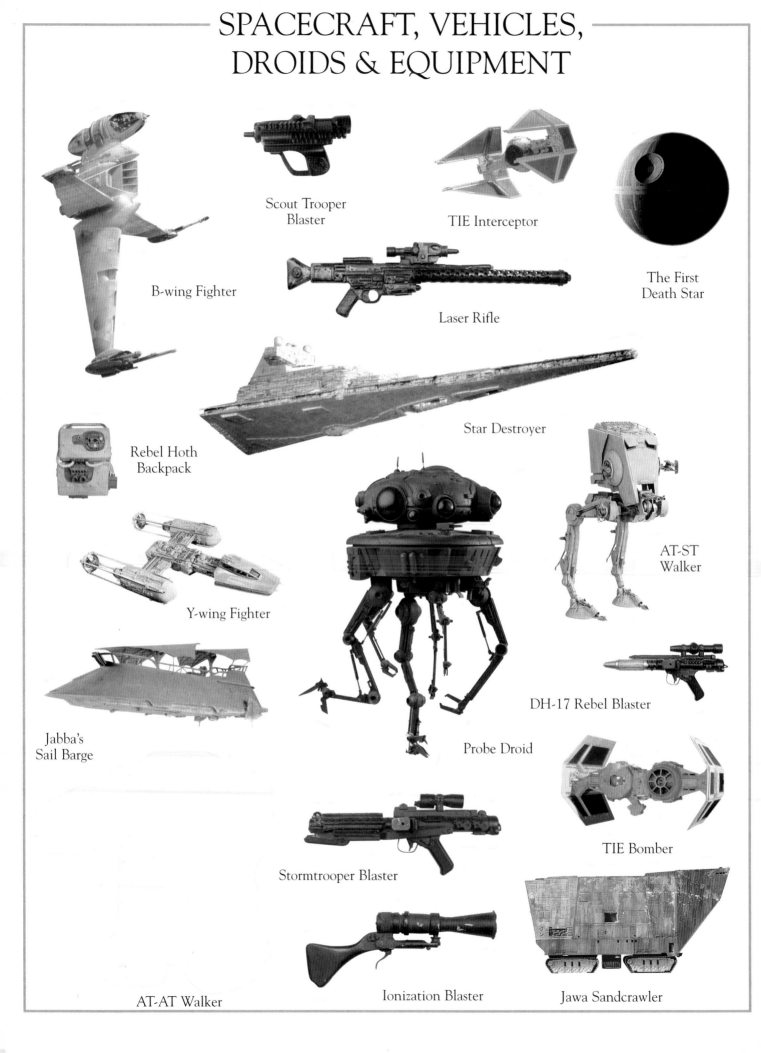

Scout Trooper Blaster

TIE Interceptor

The First Death Star

B-wing Fighter

Laser Rifle

Star Destroyer

Rebel Hoth Backpack

AT-ST Walker

Y-wing Fighter

DH-17 Rebel Blaster

Jabba's Sail Barge

Probe Droid

TIE Bomber

Stormtrooper Blaster

AT-AT Walker

Ionization Blaster

Jawa Sandcrawler

CHARACTERS & CREATURES

Boba Fett

Obi-Wan Kenobi

Tusken
Raider

Luke Skywalker

Han
Solo

Princess
Leia

Darth
Vader

Bib
Fortuna

Emperor Palpatine

Admiral Ackbar

Jabba the Hutt

CHARACTERS & CREATURES

Chewbacca

Gamorrean
Guard

Ewok

Dengar and IG-88

Imperial
Royal
Guard

Stormtrooper

Bossk and 4-LOM

Rancor

Lando
Calrissian

Yoda

Scout Trooper

Max Rebo

Jawa

Modal Nodes

SPACECRAFT, VEHICLES, DROIDS & EQUIPMENT

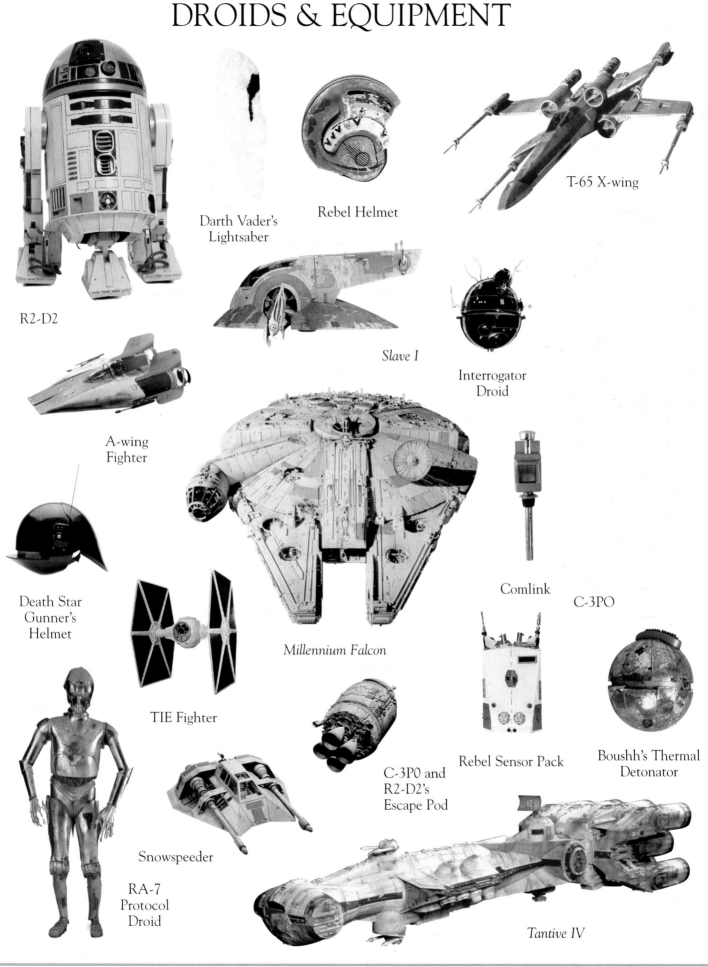

R2-D2

Darth Vader's
Lightsaber

Rebel Helmet

T-65 X-wing

Slave I

Interrogator
Droid

A-wing
Fighter

Death Star
Gunner's
Helmet

TIE Fighter

Millennium Falcon

Comlink

C-3PO

Rebel Sensor Pack

Boushh's Thermal
Detonator

C-3PO

C-3PO and
R2-D2's
Escape Pod

Snowspeeder

RA-7
Protocol
Droid

Tantive IV

Stalking Ship
Boba Fett's deceptive starship, *Slave I*, is fitted with a stolen secret sensor-masking device, enabling it to disappear from most scanning systems.

Sand Patrol
Rusted and scoured by countless sandstorms, the Jawa sandcrawler searches the wastelands of Tatooine for lost droids and salvagable junk.

Criminal Minds
Bossk is a reptilian Trandoshan and a tough bounty hunter. 4-LOM was once a sophisticated protocol droid, but has degraded to become a criminal.

Fearsome Carnivore
Kept in a pit by Jabba the Hutt, the fearsome rancor is five metres (16 feet) tall and has an armored skin.

Sand Creature
Prowling through the dunes and wastes of Tatooine, Tusken Raiders are masters of the desert. Savage and violent, they can survive where no one else can.

Tough Guard
Brutish, stubborn, and often violent, the Gamorrean guards protect Jabba's palace. They prefer to use hand-to-hand combat weapons instead of blasters.

Scavengers
Dressed in dark robes, the notoriously tricky Jawas patrol the dunes looking for junk to repair and trade.

Killer Instincts
Trained as an Imperial assassin, Dengar had brain surgery that turned him into a merciless killer. The IG-88 assassin droid is no less vile: It escaped from the laboratories and now stalks the galaxy, obsessed with killing.

Hungry Player
The crazy keyboard player, Max Rebo, is a blue Ortoloan. He is so obsessed with food that he asked Jabba to pay him in free meals.

Fearsome Criminal
As Jabba's chief lieutenant, the conniving Bib Fortuna uses underhanded methods to gain control. Despite his obsequious manner, he is always plotting a way to kill his boss.

The Rebellion

Fighting to rid the galaxy of Imperial tyranny, the Rebel Alliance relies on the light side of the Force. The Rebels are a diverse group made up of royalty, exiled aliens, droids, ex-smugglers, and Jedi Knights. Together they try to overcome the evil powers of darkness.

Steady Fire
Designed by Admiral Ackbar, the B-wing fighter has an unusual gyrostabilization system that keeps the cockpit steady while the pilot fires at the enemy.

Communication
Comlinks enable individual soldiers to communicate with other Rebels while on patrol or performing other military duties.

Young Hero
Determined and innovative, the heroic Luke Skywalker transformed himself from farmboy to wing commander for the Alliance. His natural ability to respond to the Force means he is a born leader, with the qualities to become a noble Jedi Knight.

Stern Beauty
Strong-willed, disciplined, and beautiful, Princess Leia is the youngest-ever Galactic Senator and has her own consular ship, *Tantive IV*. She uses her powerful position to help the Rebel Alliance.

Action Man
Confident, rugged, and reckless, Han Solo has worked his way up from poor beginnings to become captain of the Falcon. His gunfighting skills make him a match for any adversary.

Hard Target
The Incom T-47 airspeeder, nicknamed snowspeeder, is used for low atmospheric duty. It can reach more than 1,000 km (620 miles) per hour, and although it has no shield, its compact size makes it hard to hit.

Hoth Essentials
On the ice planet Hoth, Rebels must carry all their equipment in a special backpack.

Energy Blaster
The DH-17 Rebel blaster uses high energy blaster gases to shoot bolts of light energy.

Ocean Friend
Commander of the Rebel fleet, the cautious Admiral Ackbar comes from the ocean world of Mon Calamari. His ships, the giant Mon Cal star cruisers, are the largest in the Rebel fleet.

Mysterious Hermit
Once a great warrior of the Old Republic, the mysterious Ben Kenobi is a Jedi Knight who lives in the Jundland Wastes. His vast powers and knowledge of the Force make him a threat to the Empire.

Escape Route
This simple escape pod can propel C-3PO and R2-D2 away from danger with its basic rocket engine.

Speed Machine
Ideal for hit-and-run missions, the lightweight A-wing fighter was designed to outrun any Imperial ship.

Etiquette Master
As a protocol droid fluent in more than six million forms of communication, C-3PO is programmed to ensure that everything runs smoothly. Although he is often overwhelmed by the turbulent times, he always remains faithful to his masters.

Head Gear
The insulated Rebel helmet is marked with the Alliance symbol.

Mighty Wookiee
Rescued from slavery by Han Solo, the mighty Wookiee Chewbacca uses his mechanical skills to keep Solo's spaceship flying. He is fiercely loyal and a perfect fighting partner for Han Solo.

Loyal Servant
The quirky R2-D2 was designed as a sophisticated computer repair and information retrieval droid. He is always prepared to risk destruction to help his masters.

Rebel Craft

To survive the terrifying power of the Empire, the Rebel Alliance needs a vast range of fighter ships, special equipment, and perhaps most importantly, expert advice.

Rogue Leader
The stylish Lando Calrissian, once a roguish smuggler captain, is the flamboyant leader of Cloud City. He has a head for business and skillful judgment in battle.

Premier Fighter
One of the most impressive fighters in the Rebel force, the T-65 X-wing is extremely durable. Designed to carry heavy weapons, it is also remarkably maneuverable.

Furry Friends
Small and furry, the resourceful Ewoks live in the forests of the emerald moon, Endor.

Computer Pack
The Rebel sensor pack is fitted with a range cycle computer and a stentronic wave monitor.

High Maintenance
Despite its battered and aging appearance, Han Solo's Millennium Falcon is one of the fastest ships in the galaxy.

Durable Fighter
Before the introduction of the X-wing starfighter, the Y-wing was the main fighter for the Alliance. Built to last, it is still widely used as a combination fighter and light bomber.

Wise Teacher
At almost 900 years old, Jedi Master Yoda is very powerful with the Force. It is his duty to try and instill in Luke a faith, peace, and harmony that will protect him from the evil powers of the dark side.

Royal Ship
Princess Leia's consular ship *Tantive IV* has a traditional ship design and can be easily disguised among galactic traffic.